ALSO AVAILABLE

Adventure Time Vol 1

Adventure Time Vol 2

Adventure Time Vol 3

Adventure Time:
Vol 1 Mathematical Edition

Adventure Time:
Vol 2 Mathematical Edition

Adventure Time:
Sugary Shorts

Adventure Time:
Marceline & The Scream Queens

Adventure Time:
Playing with Fire

ADVENTURE TIME WITH FIONNA AND CAKE — Published by Titan Comics, a division of Titan Publishing Group Ltd., 144 Southwark St., London, SE1 0UP. Originally published in single comic form as ADVENTURE TIME WITH FIONNA AND CAKE 1-6. ADVENTURE TIME, CARTOON NETWORK, the logos, and all related characters and elements are trademarks of and © Cartoon Network. (S13) All rights reserved. All characters, events and institutions depicted herein are fictional. Any similarity between any of the names, characters, persons, events and/or institutions in this publication to actual names, characters, and persons, whether living or dead and/or institutions are unintended and purely coincidental.

A CIP catalogue record for this title is available from the British Library.

Printed in China.

First published in the USA and Canada in September 2013 by Kaboom!, an imprint of BOOM! Studios.

10 9 8 7 6 5 4.

ISBN: 9781782760528

www.titan-comics.com

"ADVENTURE TIME" CREATED BY

Pendleton Ward

WRITTEN AND ILLUSTRATED BY

Natasha Allegri

Colors by Natasha Allegri & Patrick Seery

with Betty Liang (Chapter 6)

LETTERS BY

Britt Wilson

"THE SWEATER BANDIT"
WRITTEN AND ILLUSTRATED BY
Noelle Stevenson

"COOTIE POWER"
WRITTEN AND ILLUSTRATED BY
Lucy Knisley

"SOUR CANDY"
WRITTEN AND ILLUSTRATED BY
Kate Leth

COVER BY
Natasha Allegri
Colors by Amanda Thomas

ASSISTANT EDITOR
Whitney Leopard

EDITOR
Shannon Watters

TRADE DESIGN BY
Stephanie Gonzaga
with Hannah Nance Partlow

With Special Thanks to Marisa Marionakis, Rick Blanco, Curtis Lelash,
Laurie Halal-Ono, Keith Mack, Kelly Crews and the
wonderful folks at Cartoon Network.

A long time ago...

...before
most things
existed...

...there was a
woman made
out of

Fire.

She lived alone...

...in a desert covered
in sand and boulders...

One day, she
discovered...

...if she
kissed a
boulder...

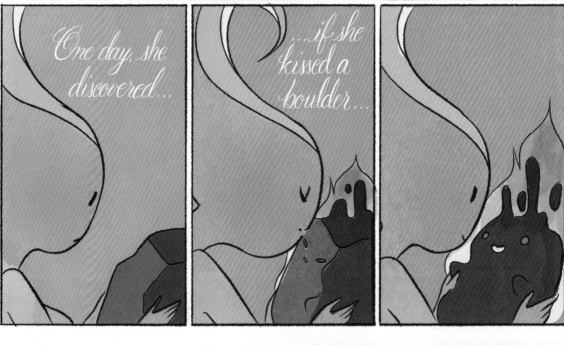

...her flames would melt it,
turning it into
a little happy
molten baby.

And she was
no longer **alone**.

For a long time, she loved and
protected all of them
like a mother...

...until the first
time it ever

RAINED.

Each raindrop that hit her weakened and shrank her...

...until her molten babies towered over her...

...and realized it was their turn to protect her.

They gathered around her, shielding her from the rain...

...but it transformed them back into their original boulder form.

And even though she's safe,
she's trapped,
and her lava tears fill up her home
and flow out into the sea...

...creating places for new life to live on.

Want me to do that thing you like where I make myself look like a big pile of doo-doo?

Yeah...

That's pretty cute.

Shapeshifting is neat, but I wish I could... SMELLSHIFT!

I wish monsoon season was over...

Whaaa...?

whoa!!!

Is the sun rising in the middle of the night?!

AAAH! Baby fire lions!
Why are they out in the rain? It's hurting them!
It looks like they're running from something...

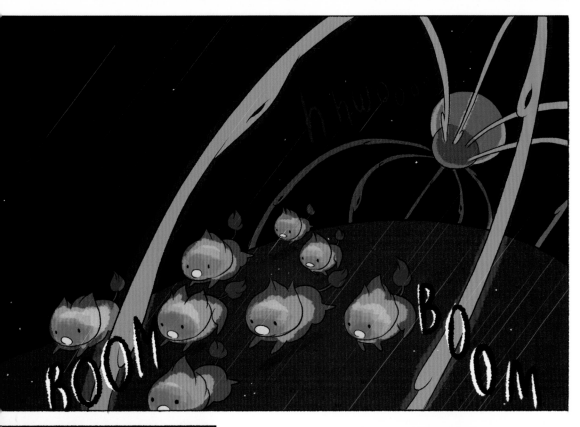

AAAHAHA HAHAHA!

ZAPP

ZIP

ZAP

ZOP

THIS'LL TEACH YOU TO STAY OUT OF MY SNOW BANKS!

HA HA
HA--

ICE
QUEEN!

Ice Queen, you better get OUTTA HERE, LADY!
whoa...
And Fionna, You better not be checkin' that guy out!
AHHH!!!!

Ahh, the rain is stopping...
Let those hot little babies go, Ice Queen!
GRRR!

OOF!

ACK!

thud

thud

PLEH.

WHA....?

ONE LITTLE HIT AND YOUR SWORD BREAKS? WHAT A POOPY SWORD!

It's kitty-litter. Of **course** it's poopy!

It's SUPER POOPY.

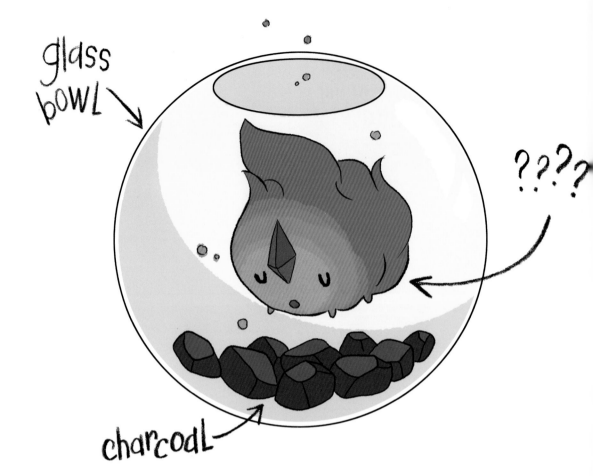

He says he needs
to find his Lion Pride so he
can protect his family's
babies from the rain
and the Ice Queen 'til
monsoon season is over...

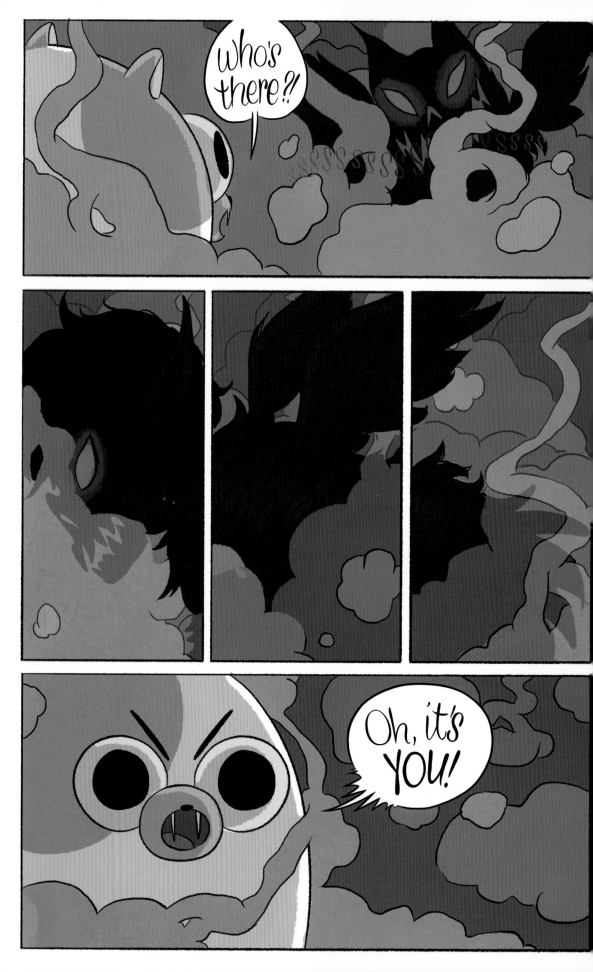

FIONNA...

Oh! Marshall Lee!

...I NEED YOUR HELP!

BOY'S NIGHT WENT HORRIBLY WRONG!

Get outta here!

CAKE, PLEASE.

You guys did boy's night without me?

Squish

FIONNA, GUMBALL IS IN TROUBLE.

HE'S STUCK IN A DUNGEON, AND YOU'RE THE ONLY ONE WHO CAN SAVE HIM.

...

...

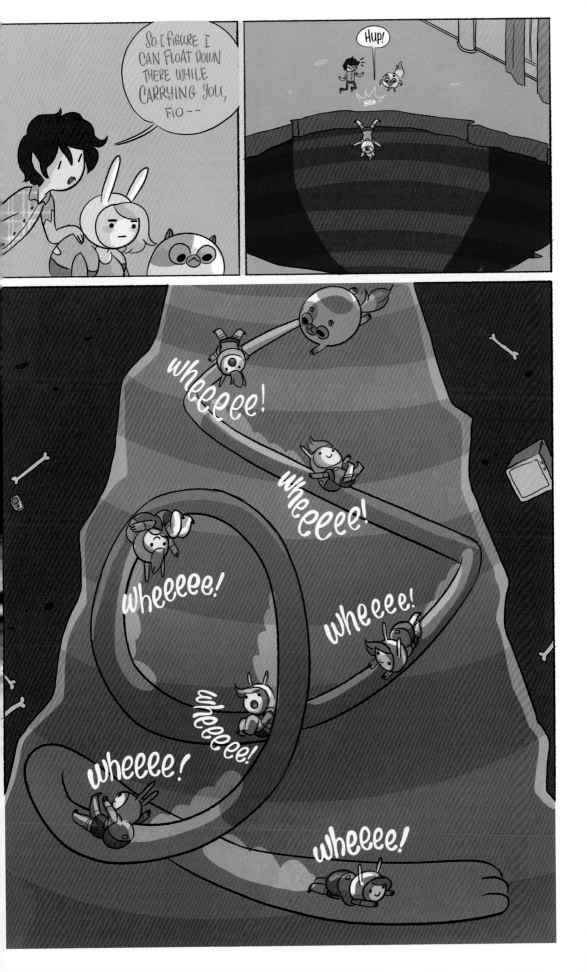

PLOP

THIS WAY...

Oh, it's cuter than I thought it would be in here.

O...KAY

kukukuku

FIONNA!! HELP!

CAKE!

Drop my Cake you dorks!

GRRR!

POP

GRAAAH!

CLACK

YAAAUGGH!

STOMP STOMP

Fionna...?

You're awake!

Fionna, you saved me...

Why didn't you guys invite me to boy's night?

...

...

You guys usually always invite me!

If I was here I would have been able to save you right away! I just wanna protect you guys from puddings and candy skulls and--

EEEEEH...

ALRIGHT GUMBALL, LET'S NOT HIDE IT FROM HER ANYMORE,

IT'S JUST MAKIN' HER SAD.

Okay, okay, you're right...

...

Oh.

There's a legend about an amazing sacred artifact that can create beautiful... magical... powerful items... but only a very skilled individual...

...can actually use this artifact... and after generations of neglect, the relic was lost to the Candy Kingdom.

But I've spent my whole life searching for it... and learning how to use this magical furnace...

...and now...

...I'm finally ready.

I'm finally going to use the Ancient Enchanted Oven...

...I had only heard of in bedtime stories!

To be on the
cusp of

IMPOSSIBLE BEAUTY

has been my curse
since the day I was born...

Uhhhhgh...

I'm...alive?

CAPTURE THE PRINCE!

Wait! Stop!

I know you think Lumpy Space Prince is good lookin' now, but don't let him manipulate your maiden hearts with his weird handsomeness!

I know that a beautiful man can turn any lady into a beast...

... but I also know, deep down inside, you're all kind, caring, thoughtful creatures.

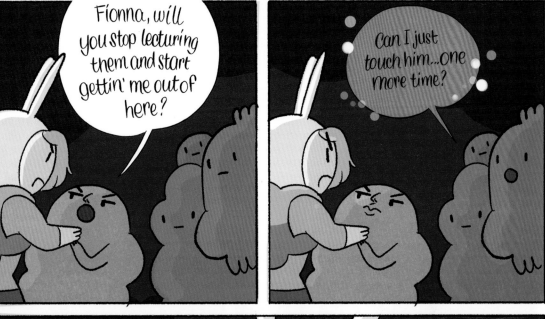

FWOOSH

WAUUUUGHHHHH!

HWA HWA HWA!!

Hooo! HOOOO HOooo!

YOWWL!

Ah!

Cake! Stop! Puttin' out his fire, it's hurtin' him!

Are you okay?

FIONNA! STOP!

beep!

What? I could touch him before!

Exactly, I nuked him in the oven to raise his body temperature.

At midnight he'll cool down and return to his weakened form...

fwoosh!

fwoosh!

...but right now he's too hot to handle.

Don't be sad! Besides, I've got a pretty matching outfit for you to wear too!

Awww man...

...it's not another moonlight princess dress is it?

IF I HAD KNOWN YOU WERE ROYALTY, LIKE MYSELF, I WOULD HAVE DEFINITELY **NOT** BEATEN UP YOUR LITTLE BUDDIES.

BUT I'M GLAD YOU AGREED TO MEET UP WITH ME FOR A—

TURN...

I GUESS IT'S A DOUBLE DATE WITH ONE OF YOUR UGLIER FIRE LIONS.

COME ON IN, I'VE PREPARED A DINNER BY CANDLELIGHT.

*poo
**HAW HAW!

A cat that didn't hate water...

...saved from drowning by a river nymph.

And when the cat found out the very mortal river nymph was in love with an immortal...

...she said,

"As a cat, I've lived five lives now, and I've seen and heard of a lost treasure that can help you live forever, too."

But the river nymph declined,

"My mortality is what makes all of this so precious to me."

The water nymph had followed to keep the cat safe.

Realizing how injured she was, the cat cried,

"You've saved me twice now, please let me help you!"

When the cat didn't get a response...

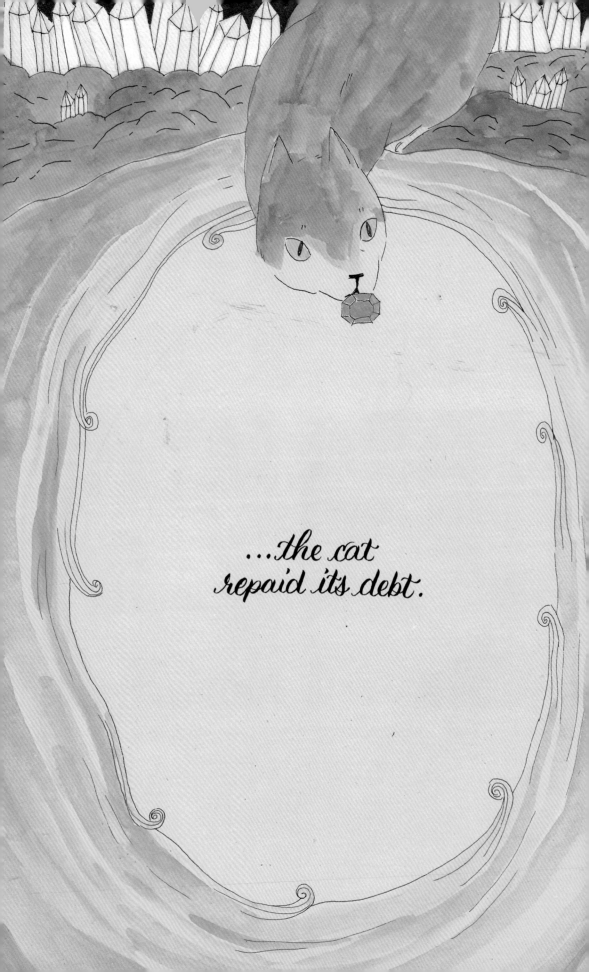

...the cat
repaid its debt.

I THOUGHT WHAT I NEEDED WAS THE LOVE OF A PRINCE...

... UNTIL I FOUND THESE FLAME ELEMENTALS.

BUT THIS CRYSTAL MANAGED TO HARNESS EVEN MORE WARMTH THAN THE BOTH OF THOSE COMBINED.

Vyoom

Ping

She's melting.

Wha...

Cake, how do you know that?

CRK

CRK

CRK

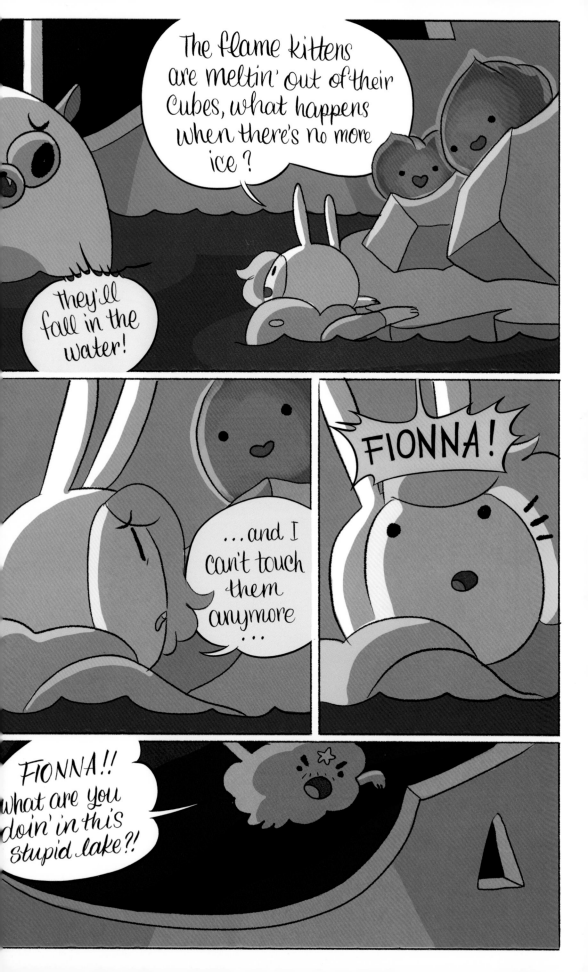

Listen, I tried bein' nice, but I'm still not like, **PHYSICALLY** hot, So I want that wand back.

LSP, I don't have time for this, I --

Sorry Fionna, after he forced me to tell him where you were, he dragged me along.

GGGRRAWWW

CRK!

AH, IT'S TRYING TO MAKE OUT WITH ME!!

CHOMP!

Hey, you've got one more wish button on your wand left!

You can use it to turn into a fire princess, and we can go down there and you guys can hang out more! I can teach you cat, and—

Ummm... nah...

Sweet Shorts

the SWEATER BANDIT by Noelle Stevenson

Brrr, it's really chilly today!

you Know what that means, girl!

It's-

SWEATER TIME!

Hey! Where's our sweaters?

Aw man, I Know they were in here!

They must have been PILFERED!

Look, Fionna!

A whole trail of sweater Fuzzies!

I bet they'll lead us right to the pilferer!

Come on! we need to get our sweaters back before we catch COLDS!

Hey! There's Prince Gumball!

Fionna! Thank Glob you're here!

someone has absconded with my sweaters!

It's too cold for my normal clothes— BUT NOT COLD ENOUGH FOR MY PARKA.

Hi guys, whatcha doin'?

Hey Marshall Lee, did your sweaters go missing too?

No way! I'm a vampire, I don't get cold!

WELL THAT'S JUST GREAT FOR YOU

I did see a guy going into that cave over there with a bunch of sweaters, though.

THE PILFERER!

Let's go get our stuff back, dudes!

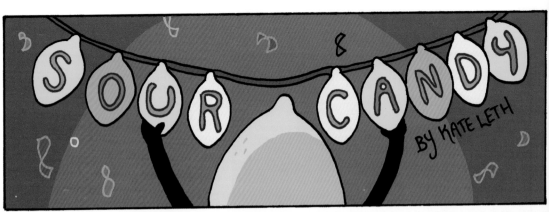

cootie power

Evil fiends, potatoes, beans... ♪

...The greatest spleens I ever seens! ♪

...Sardines! ♪

SNIFF

Fionna, when was the last time you had a bath?

Who knows?

Who cares?

HUFF Hu

I do! I can smell your smell and it is SMELLY!

You're just sensitive because of your cat nose.

OH MY GLOB FIONNA

Huff Huff

You'll never... (huff)... guess what... (pant) just—

SNIFF

Eew, is that you!?

What is it, Lumpy Space Prince?

Alright, whatever stinkball...

You probably have COOTIES but FINÉ.

YES!

Hm.

Fionna! You saved us!

Saved by the power of smell!

Sorry about earlier.

In fact, I decree that nobody in the land shall bathe more than you do!

For SAFETY!

Nice!

On second thought...

Um...

RRRUMBLE

POUR

Finally!

This is the best way to get clean!

Where ya goin?

After: See, no smell!

Right this way!

COOTIE CAM

THE END.

Cover Gallery

Issue #1A
Jen Bennett
Colors by Lisa Moore

Issue #1B
Joe Quinones

Issue #IC
Vera Brosgol

Issue #ID
Ethan Rilly

Issue #IE
Becky Dreistadt
& Frank Gibson

Issue #1 Hastings Exclusive
Sina Grace
Colors by S. Steven Struble

Issue #1 Emerald City
Comicon Exclusive
Colleen Coover

Issue #1 Awesome Con Exclusive
Penelope Gaylord
Colors by Kassandra Heller

Issue #1 Dynamic
Forces Exclusive
Emily Warren

Issue #1 Web Exclusive
Stephanie Gonzaga

Issue #1 San Diego
Comic-Con Exclusive
Natasha Allegri

Issue #1 Phantom Exclusive
& Larry's Comics
Yssa Badiola

Issue #1 Second Printing
Stephanie Gonzaga

Issue #2A
Chad Thomas
Colors by Zack Sterling

Issue #2B
Rebecca Mock

Issue #2C
Stephanie Buscema

Issue #2D
Maris Wicks

Issue #2 Second Printing
Stephanie Gonzaga

Issue #2 Phantom Exclusive
& Larry's Comics
Charles Paul Wilson III

Issue #2 Web Exclusive
Stephanie Gonzaga

Issue #3A
Natasha Allegri
Colors by Amanda Thomas

Issue #3B
Zack Sterling

Issue #3C
Lea Hernandez

Issue #3D
Abby Boeh

Issue #3 Phantom Exclusive
& Larry's Comics
Kel McDonald

Issue #3 Web Exclusive
Stephanie Gonzaga

Issue #4B
Terry Blas &
Kimball Davis

Issue #4C
Rachel Dukes

Issue #4D
Faith Erin Hicks
Colors by Noreen Rana

Issue #4A
Natasha Allegri

Issue #4 Calgary Expo
Exclusive
Shoichi Uehara

Issue #4 Phantom Exclusive
& Larry's Comics
Matt Talbot

Issue #5C
Gigi D.G.

Issue #5A
Natasha Allegri
Colors by Amanda Thomas

Issue #5B
Coleman Engle

Issue #5D
Chrystin Garland

Issue #5 Heroes Con Exclusive
Andy Hirsch

Issue #5 Phantom Exclusive
& Larry's Comics
Matt Talbot

Issue #5 Web Exclusive
Stephanie Gonzaga

Issue #6A
Natasha Allegri

Issue #6B
Jen Wang

Issue #6C
Rachel Saunders

Issue #6D
Kate Leth

Issue #6 Phantom Exclusive
& Larry's Comics
Matt Talbot

Issue #6 Cards, Comics,
& Collectibles Exclusive
Nomi Kane

Issue #6 Web Exclusive
Stephanie Gonzaga

Issue #6 San Diego
Comic-Con Exclusive
Kassandra Heller